We've cast a spell, there's joy to share,
With friends of fairies everywhere!
Open this enchanted book,
Make a wish and take a look.

Inside there are all kinds of things,
It's time to find your fairy wings!
You'll read and make and play all day,
It's the Rainbow Magic way!

This spellbinding
2012 Annual
belongs to

.....Kate!..............

ORCHARD BOOKS
338 Euston Road, London NW1 3BH
Orchard Books Australia
Level 17/207 Kent Street, Sydney, NSW 2000

First published in 2011 by Orchard Books.

A CIP catalogue record for this book is available
from the British Library.

ISBN 978 1 40831 282 7

1 3 5 7 9 10 8 6 4 2

Printed in Italy
Orchard Books is a division of Hachette Children's Books,
an Hachette UK company

www.hachette.co.uk

Annual
2012

Step into Fairyland...

Contents

Enchanted Pet S.O.S.

Hello! It's so lovely to meet you, especially here in the 2012 Rainbow Magic Annual! This year King Oberon and Queen Titania asked everyone in Fairyland to share their most magical spells, tips and make-its ever.

Unfortunately, Jack Frost wants to spoil everything as usual, and has stolen the Pet Keeper Fairies' special friends! We think he has hidden them in this book. Can you find them all?

Thank you, dear friend!
Kirsty & Rachel xxx

Pet Passport
NAME:
Misty
BELONGS TO:
Bella the Bunny Fairy
Found on page: ?

Pet Passport
NAME:
Sparky
BELONGS TO:
Georgia the Guinea Pig Fairy
Found on page: ?

Pet Passport
NAME:
Shimmer
BELONGS TO:
Katie the Kitten Fairy
Found on page:

Pet Passport
NAME:
Glitter
BELONGS TO:
Penny the Pony Fairy
Found on page: ?

Pet Passport
NAME:
Flash
BELONGS TO:
Molly the Goldfish Fairy
Found on page: ?

Pet Passport
NAME:
Twinkle
BELONGS TO:
Harriet the Hamster Fairy
Found on page: ?

Pet Passport
NAME:
Sunny
BELONGS TO:
Lauren the Puppy Fairy
Found on page: ?

Answers can be found on page 61!

7

Shivery spot-the-Difference

The mention of Jack Frost's name always puts a chill in the air, but not all fairies mind icy winds and heavy skies. Crystal the Snow Fairy works hard to create glittering snow showers all winter long, and when Storm the Lightning Fairy waves her wand thunderbolts rumble and flash, clearing the air for a bright new day.

Take a look at these stunning pictures of Crystal and Storm. Can you spot seven differences?

If you're finding this tricky, don't forget that all the answers are waiting for you at the back of the book!

Meet Katie the Kitten Fairy

Draw Shimmer in Katie's arms.

I love playing hide and seek with my cute magic kitten!

Personality
Curious, playful and independent.

Animal companion
Shimmer. She's a fluffy baby pussycat with white and grey fur.

Favourite colour
Creamy-white.

What Katie loves best about kittens
Their pink paddy paws! She was so thrilled when Shimmer chose her as a fairy keeper!

Most trusted magic
In a flash of amber sparkles, Shimmer can change her size and shape.

Yummiest food
Some milk and a tuna sandwich – like Shimmer! Though Shimmer would leave the bread.

Shimmer really is an incredible little cat. She can magically change herself into a fierce striped tiger and back again before Katie can even say the words 'sparkly spells'!

I found Shimmer on page ....

Fairy outfit
Katie's glossy black hair is fixed in place with a pair of miniature butterfly clips. Her strapless dress has a layered skirt that floats beautifully when she flutters through the air. The hem of the gauzy yellow silk has been painted rose-petal pink.

9

Make a Party Piñata!

Belle the Birthday Fairy flutters all over Fairyland, making sure that everyone has a wonderful time on their birthday! For extra-special occasions, she likes to surprise her friends with a party piñata. Would you like to make one too?

Belle's colourful piñata is covered in pretty frills of crepe paper. When the birthday girl and her friends tap the piñata with a bat, all sorts of lovely things will spill out from inside!

First collect...

A balloon
50g flour
Measuring jug
Old newspapers, torn into strips
Paintbrush
Coloured poster paint
Bright strips of crepe paper
PVA glue
Scissors
Pencil
Household string

1 Blow up your balloon then ask a grown-up to tie a knot in the end.

2 Measure the flour into a plastic bowl, then stir in 150ml of tap water. Give the mixture a good stir – this will be the glue that holds your piñata together!

3 Dip strips of newspaper into the glue, then lay them on the balloon. Keep draping on pieces of paper until the entire balloon is covered.

4 When the balloon has dried out, paste on a second and then a third layer of newspaper. Make sure you allow plenty of time between building up each new layer, so that the paste can set properly.

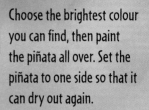

5 Choose the brightest colour you can find, then paint the piñata all over. Set the piñata to one side so that it can dry out again.

5

6 When the piñata is dry, ask a grown-up to pop the balloon inside.

7 Wind an eye-catching strip of crepe paper around the top of the piñata, dotting PVA glue along the upper edge. Work your way down, sticking more rows of crepe in place. When you reach the bottom your piñata should be completely trimmed with pretty frills!

8 Ask a grown-up to push a pencil through the top of the piñata at either side of the hole made by the balloon. Loop a piece of string through the small holes, then tie it in a knot to make a hook. Now it's party time!

7

Let's Play Piñata!

Put lots of tiny sweets, toys and surprises into the hole at the top of your piñata. Ask an adult helper to hang up the piñata in your party room. Put on some music, then invite your friends to take turns tapping the piñata with the end of a broomstick. Sooner or later your pretty make-it will break, showering you all with treats.

Meet Flora the Fancy Dress Fairy

Flora the Fancy Dress Fairy simply clicks her fingers to create the perfect costume for any party theme!

My magic makes sure that fancy dress parties go without a hitch!

Personality
Creative, giggly and sweet.

Happiest hobby
Trying on big hats, stitching clothes and planning parties.

Favourite colour
Deep emerald, like the rolling ocean.

Favourite fairy playmate
Ashley the Dragon Fairy.

Most trusted magic
Her spells turn old clothes into stunning costumes, each one more amazing than the last.

Yummiest food
Kiwi fruit, spring rolls and scented jelly.

Jack Frost was about to spoil a grand fancy dress ball at McKersey Castle, when Flora fluttered in to save the day! Kirsty and Rachel had a wonderful time at the party. They dressed up in gorgeous angel costumes and carried real silver harps.

Fairy outfit
Flora changes her outfit all the time! At the moment, her favourite is this stunning turquoise mermaid costume. It has a shimmering tail skirt that catches the light whenever she moves. Flora's greeny-blue tumble of curls is topped off with a crown of shells.

Flora's Fancy Dress Party

Flora would like to help you find your dream fancy dress costume! The kindly fairy has waved her wand across this page, filling it with wonderful skirts, masks and headdresses! Colour in the outfit you'd most like to wear, using your favourite shades.

Return to Rainspell Island

After Kirsty and Rachel's first adventure on Rainspell Island, the girls had proved that they were true friends of the Rainbow Fairies...

Kirsty and Rachel hugged. They had only known each other for a few days, but they were best friends already! Saving the Rainbow Fairies from Jack Frost had been an amazing way to get to know each other.

Ruby the Red Fairy and her sisters were thrilled to be together again. They invited Kirsty and Rachel to Fairyland so King Oberon and Queen Titania could thank them properly. Ruby waved her wand, and the girls shrank down to fairy-size!

Suddenly the skies went dark – Jack Frost and his goblins appeared! The Ice Lord was determined to capture the frightened fairies before they could make their kingdom colourful again. Shards of ice flew out of his magic staff, pinning all seven to the spot.

Kirsty and Rachel managed to trick the goblins, then seize Jack Frost's staff. The wicked Ice Lord was sent back to Fairyland in a snowglobe prison! King Oberon and Queen Titania gave the girls magic amulets to say thank you for putting the colours back into their world.

14

When Kirsty went to stay with Rachel during the next school holidays, their adventure with the Rainbow Fairies seemed like a faraway dream. They both secretly hoped for another chance to meet their seven tiny friends.

One day, on a walk around the shops in Tippington, Kirsty and Rachel bumped into some bullies from Rachel's school. Lydia and her nasty friends burst into fits of laughter when they overheard that the girls believed in fairies. They sneered and called them babies.

Later that afternoon, Rachel's mum told the girls that they were off to Rainspell Island again for a Nature Guide camp! Kirsty couldn't help notice Rachel's face fall when she discovered that Lydia and her pals would be coming too.

While the Nature Guides put up their tents, King Oberon was taking pity on Jack Frost. He decided to release him from his snowglobe, as long as he promised to go straight back to his Ice Castle until it was the proper time for winter to begin.

As soon as he was back in his frozen kingdom, Jack Frost started to plot. For him, being good meant being the best bad ever! He struck the ice with his magic staff. At that very instant a snowman was formed, then another and another. It was the start of a snowman army!

Super Sporty Wordsearch

Helena, Francesca, Zoe, Naomi, Samantha, Alice and Gemma are getting ready to go out and play some games! Help the fairies off to a flying start by finding all the sporty objects hiding in this wordsearch grid.

Look closely at the letters, drawing a line round every item you spot. Don't forget that the words could be running in any direction – up, down, left, right or diagonally!

Words
It's
really
not
fairy
words

Bike
Netball
Snowboard
Trainers
Football Top
Goggles
Jodhpurs
Tennis Racket
Bib
Oar
Swimsuit
Leotard
Kneepads

F	O	O	T	B	A	L	L	T	O	P	S
S	D	A	P	E	E	N	K	A	T	Q	W
W	P	B	M	B	Z	G	M	J	B	C	I
X	F	J	S	I	V	G	O	I	Y	I	M
L	K	F	D	R	Z	K	B	I	K	E	S
E	Z	D	V	S	E	J	T	R	Q	M	U
O	A	R	K	N	T	N	W	C	B	P	I
T	E	K	C	A	R	S	I	N	N	E	T
A	I	D	X	C	V	Q	M	A	H	X	Z
R	I	J	J	O	D	H	P	U	R	S	S
D	S	N	O	W	B	O	A	R	D	T	O
G	O	G	G	L	E	S	R	J	S	D	L
L	L	A	B	T	E	N	G	I	V	D	Z

Answers can be found on page 61!

Sweet Little Mystery

A shy but utterly delightful fairy is hiding in the shadows! Can you work out who she might be, then coax her back into the light? Read each of the clues, study her silhouette, then write her name in the special frame at the bottom of the page!

I have big brown eyes.

Juliet

It's my job to make sure that February 14th is full of love and happiness!

I wear a pink jumper and a denim skirt with two hearts stitched on the front.

J E F A U R
A J T N E U T
A I T W N E V I E
L L Y H

Need a shimmer of inspiration? All the letters in this heart spell out the fairy's name.

The fairy is

JULIET THE

Valentine fairy

Uncover the Magic!

If you were a fairy, what sort of magic do you think you might be put in charge of? When King Oberon and Queen Titania give out the jobs in Fairyland they choose an enchanted task that will suit each new fairy's personality.

The chart will lead you to your true fairy destiny!

Starting in the big heart on the left, first draw a line of sparkles to connect the words you like the best, then choose the heart that describes you in a single word. Try not to think too long about each step, just follow your heart!

rainbows

secrets

fairydust

snowflakes

spells

magic wands

I like...

sunshine

giggles

fluttery wings

moonbeams

daydreams

tiny tiaras

26

I would describe myself as...

hopeful

brave

caring

funny

kind-hearted

creative

ociable

You show many of the same qualities as Leona the Unicorn Fairy. If you were a fairy a flash of your wand would heal unwell people and animals too!

You've got a strong heart, just like Caitlin the Ice Bear Fairy! Your natural magic would spread courage – standing up to bullies and righting wrongs all over the world!

Only a very special girl or fairy has the power to spread compassion. You and Sophia the Snow Swan Fairy show friends how to be kind to each other in a hundred different ways!

You and Rihanna the Seahorse Fairy will never be lonely. Your secret enchantment is the power to bring friends together wherever you go!

There's a secret in your step – you're a walking lucky charm, just like Lara the Black Cat Fairy! Good things just seem to come your way, no matter what you do.

You and Erin the Firebird Fairy have so much in common! Your faces light up every time you smile or laugh. Your magical sense of humour is impossible to resist!

You're a natural dreamer, and no wonder – there are so many amazing things floating around inside your head! You and Ashley the Dragon Fairy have a truly magical imagination.

The Party Fairy A to Z!

The Party Fairies are experts at making celebrations turn out beautifully each and every time. Now they've written an alphabet of party ideas to make your next fairy gathering the best one yet!

A is for Arts & crafts

Fairies love making things together! Print out Rainbow Magic pictures for your guests to colour in or use glue to decorate pretty hair bands that your friends can wear home.

B is for Body glitter

Make yourself shimmer and shine for your party guests! Smooth a dusting of glitter over your arms and shoulders so that you catch the light as you move through the room.

C is for Cake

Every party should have one even if it's not a birthday celebration. Cherry believes that the best cakes are made by hand. That way you can stir love and good wishes into the mixture before you bake it in the oven!

D is for Decorations

Grace sprinkles glitter, pins up balloons and curls streamers from the ceiling. Why not drape pretty netting round the windows then pin paper butterflies or flowers onto it?

E is for Entrance

Make a big impression on your guests by decorating the door leading into the party. Fairy lights and colourful garlands will make your friends feel in the mood for magic.

F is for Fairy feast

Before you plan your menu think about the sort of occasion you are going to be hosting. Sandwiches work best for a tea party, but pizza and popcorn fit the bill when it's sleepover time!

G is for Games

The best way to get your guests chatting and giggling is to play a few fairy games! Polly the Party Fun Fairy plans out her games before everyone arrives, gathering all the things she needs.

H is for Happy smile

Always wear a big friendly smile to make each and every one of your guests feel welcome!

I is for Invitations

Send these out in plenty of time so that all your friends can save your special date on their calendars.

J is for Joining in

If you notice that one of your guests is feeling a little shy, make an effort to help her join in with the dancing and games. Soon everyone will start to have much more fun.

K is for Keepsake

Cover a plain notebook with some pretty wrapping paper then leave it open on a table. Ask each of your friends to sign the book before they go home and you'll be left with a lovely keepsake of your special day!

L is for Laughing

Parties should be fun for everyone! Don't waste time hiding in the kitchen worrying about how things will turn out – once the guests arrive it's time to have fun!

M is for Music

Set the fairy scene by playing floaty music in the background while your guests play games or eat their party tea. Burn CDs in advance with all your favourite pop tunes so that you just have to flick a switch to get the dancing started.

N is for Nibbles

While your friends wait for everyone to arrive, tempt your guests with a tray of cute party canapés. Canapés are easy to eat and the perfect size for delicate fairy fingers! There are all sorts of mouth-watering ideas on page 22.

30

O
is for Outfit

The fairy host should always be the belle of the ball! Plan a party outfit that makes you stand out from the crowd, but keeps you comfortable too.

P
is for Party workshop!

This could be your kitchen, bedroom or even your garden. It's a place where all the hard work is done, whether that's cooking, wrapping presents or making decorations!

Q
is for Queen of the Fairies

Ask each of your guests to dress up as a fairy princess, complete with tiara, gown and wings. When everyone gathers at the party, vote for the girl you'd like to be the Queen of the Fairies. She becomes queen for the day, winning a prize and starting off the dancing.

R
is for Remembering to say thank you

Fairies have impeccable manners. Always thank your guests for coming then send them a little note afterwards if you're lucky enough to receive a gift.

S
is for a Sprinkling of fairy dust

You can never have too much sparkle when you're planning a fairy celebration! Sprinkle a cascade of magic dust over each of your guests as they arrive.

T
is for Treats

Honey loves seeing her guests' faces when she gives them a special treat. Why not put a lollipop on everybody's place setting or try making the party piñata on page 10?

molty culers

U
is for Unbelievable!

Fairy wonder just gets stronger and stronger when there are lots of magical people gathered together. After you've had tea, find a lovely spot in the garden and sit hand-in-hand. Whisper your most precious secrets and share wishes for all your fairy friends.

V
is for Video

Beautiful memories should be cherished! Ask your mum or dad to film some of the important parts of the day or take snaps on their camera that you can put into an album later.

W
is for Wrapping-up

When you host a party it's fun to give each of your guests a little present when they leave. Write a happy spell for each of your friends then pop it in a party bag with a sheet of pretty stickers – such a personal gift is sure to go down a treat!

X
is for X marks the spot

A treasure hunt is a great icebreaker, especially if it's outside in the garden. Make a little fairy ring in a hidden corner, then draw out maps or a list of clues for the players to follow.

Y
is for Yawn

Variety keeps a party interesting right up to the very end. If your guests look like they've played enough games, get them up dancing. When they've danced themselves dizzy, sit in a circle and share fairy stories instead.

Z
is for Zzzz...

When the guests have gone and the cleaning-up's done, make sure you get a good rest!

Words and Wishes

Chrissie the Wish Fairy is extra busy – she has three magical objects to hide in the human world. Can you guess what they might be?

Chrissie has cleverly created a secret fairy code to tell you exactly what she's planning to hide. Find a cosy corner away from frosty windows and prying goblin eyes. Look up each code letter on the special key and then trace your finger down to the true fairy letter waiting below.

Code Letter		Fairy Letter	Code Letter		Fairy Letter	Code Letter		Fairy Letter	Code Letter		Fairy Letter
A	=	X	H	=	E	O	=	L	V	=	S
B	=	Z	I	=	F	P	=	M	W	=	T
C	=	Y	J	=	G	Q	=	N	X	=	U
D	=	A	K	=	H	R	=	O	Y	=	V
E	=	B	L	=	I	S	=	P	Z	=	W
F	=	C	M	=	J	T	=	Q			
G	=	D	N	=	K	U	=	R			

P C P D J L F D O R E M H F W V

My magical objects

D U H D F D U G, D F D U R O

Are a card, a carol

V K H H W D Q G D V S R R Q.

sheet and a spoon

34

Meet Lauren the Puppy Fairy

Draw Sunny cuddling up to Lauren the Puppy Fairy.

My magical spaniel has the waggiest tail in Fairyland!

Personality
Faithful, fun and always happy to see you!

Animal companion
Sunny. He's an adorable shaggy puppy with a glittery silver collar.

Favourite colour
Golden brown.

What Lauren loves best about puppies
Her fairy heart melts every time she looks into Sunny's big brown eyes.

Most trusted magic
Sunny can make things appear out of thin air – from bouncy balls and frisbees to sweet doggy treats!

Yummiest food
Sizzling sausages and homemade cookies pressed into puppy shapes.

Sunny loves to scamper along the ground and through the air! He gambols through the sky behind Lauren, leaving a tiny trail of fairy dust glittering behind him.

I found Sunny on page ......

Fairy outfit
Lauren's silk cargo pants are just the thing for a fluttery fairy who's always on the go! She accessorises her outfit with a stunning petal pendant and flowery hair clips – all in matching shades of pink.

Sunny Steals the Show
Part 1

It was the day that the Pet Keeper Fairies had been looking forward to all year – the Royal Pet Extravaganza! King Oberon and Queen Titania had been invited to judge a special pet show in the palace gardens. As well as the chance of winning rosettes, animals from all over Fairyland would be performing magic tricks and joining in an amazing flying finale! Lauren the Puppy Fairy felt butterflies flutter in her tummy. There were only five minutes to go before the excitement began. Could she and her little dog, Sunny, win a prize in the biggest pet show in Fairyland?

Lauren pulled a little brush from the pocket of her cargo pants and ran it through her tumbling brown hair. As she hopped nervously from foot to foot, shimmers of scarlet fairy dust tingled and popped in the air. Over on the lawn in front of her, dozens of fairies and their pets were lining up in a ring circled with garlands of rainbow-coloured ribbon.

"Good luck, Lauren," smiled Harriet the Hamster Fairy, fluttering past. Her tiny hamster, Twinkle, chirruped happily, tucked up in the crook of Harriet's arm.

"Thanks," grinned Lauren. "And you too!"

Just then, Penny the Pony Fairy rode up on Glitter, her stunning white pony.

"All set?" she winked, looking down at the clipboard she was carrying. As Pet Keeper Fairies, Lauren and her friends were in charge of organising the Extravaganza every year. Bella the Bunny Fairy had sent out all the invitations, Harriet had set the show timetable and Lauren had made a pile of gorgeous rosettes. Now Penny, Georgia, Katie and Molly were on hand to make sure that the day ran without a hitch.

"Hi, Penny!" said Lauren. "We're as ready as we'll ever be, aren't we, Sunny?" Lauren looked down, but her brown spaniel wasn't there!

"Come out, Sunny," called the Puppy Fairy, putting her hands on her hips. "Don't be nervous, I'll be with you all the time."

Lauren and Penny waited a moment. With a sudden *ping!* Sunny popped his little head out from behind a rose bush. He trotted over to Lauren and nuzzled her leg.

"A magical puppy like you will do brilliantly, I'm sure," said Penny in a kind voice. She marked a tick on her clipboard next to Sunny's name, then guided Glitter forward. "Looks like Leona the Unicorn Fairy has arrived – let's go and say hello to Twisty."

When they were alone, Lauren crouched down next to Sunny and took his paw in her hand. The devoted pet gazed back at her with adorable brown eyes. His waggy tail thumped up and down on the grass.

"Don't be shy, Sunny," she whispered. "I know you can win a rosette today! Just be yourself."

Suddenly a voice came over the loudspeakers dotted around the palace gardens – it was Bertram, the king's frog footman!

"All contestants, please take your places in the ring," he announced.

Fairies and pets of all shapes and sizes began to rush into the arena. Lauren saw Erin the Firebird Fairy skip past with her stunning bird, Giggles, perched on her arm. Tess the Sea Turtle Fairy was already in the ring, peering into a special pool that had been made for all the watery pets. Her turtle, Pearl, floated elegantly round the edge before diving below the surface.

Destiny the Pop Star Fairy

Destiny the Pop Star Fairy is getting ready to rock the fairy crowd at her annual concert! Can you colour in the magical pop princess, from her musical note-popping magic wand right down to her super-stylish wedge heels?

Now draw in Destiny's audience of fairies all dancing and singing to the beat!

Flowery Fairy Fun

Pippa the Poppy Fairy has cast a petally puzzle spell especially for you! Read each of her clues, then fill the right letters into the crossword squares. Colour in a flower for every one you solve.

Across:
1. SUNFLOWER
2. DANIELLE
3. ROSES
4. JACK
5. tulip

Down:
1. PETALS
2. LILY
3. PURPLE
4. BLOSSOMHALL
5. RAIN

Psst! If you're struggling with a clue or two, don't forget to flip to the answers on page 61.

Across

1. The tallest flower looked after by the Petal Fairies.
2. The name of the golden-haired Daisy Fairy.
3. The sweet flower tended by Ella.
4. The baddie who wants to fill his castle garden with flowers.
5. The gorgeous orange bloom that Tia watches over.

Down

1. The magical items that belong to Poppy and her friends.
2. The name of Louise's delicate bloom.
3. The colour of Olivia the Orchid Fairy's funky frock.
4. The old hotel where Kirsty and Rachel first met the Petal Fairies.
5. Wet weather that helps flowers grow.

47

Amazing Oceans

Don't you love the beautiful, briny sea? The oceans surge over massive areas of the human world, and there are countless amazing creatures living within them! When the goblins smashed Fairyland's Magical Conch Shell into seven pieces, it was no wonder that the Ocean Fairies promised to restore it – the ocean and its animals are too important to come to any harm.

Did you know?

...that penguins are birds that cannot fly. They use their wings as paddles when gliding through the water.

Did you know?

...that there are 33 species of seals in the world. Two types live around the shores of Great Britain.

Did you know?

...that bottlenose dolphins make their own unique music by blending whistles, grunts and squeaks.

Pia the Penguin Fairy

and her little friend Scamp roam the South Pole, caring for penguins who need help.

Amelie the Seal Fairy

and her gorgeous pal Silky make sure that seals all over the world stay safe.

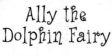

Ally the Dolphin Fairy

looks after all the dolphins with her magical friend, Echo.

Did you know?

...that Leatherback Sea Turtles are the biggest on Earth. Sometimes they stretch to over two metres long!

Did you know?

...that Orca whales travel in large family groups called pods.

Tess the Sea Turtle Fairy

swims all over the planet with her friend Pearl, caring for sea turtles and their babies.

Whitney the Whale Fairy

has a magical companion called Flukey who helps her look after the world's whales.

Did you know?

...that starfish have tiny tube feet that they use to move themselves over rocks and sand.

Water Wonderland

Water gushes over 71% of the Earth's surface – that's nearly three-quarters of the planet! From tropical beaches to the iceberg-filled poles, the oceans never cease to astound and amaze. Above the surface we can only glimpse at their wonders. Beneath the waves, an underwater world of mountains and valleys, caves and reefs stretches for countless miles.

Stephanie the Starfish Fairy

works with her tiny pal Spike to watch over starfish and rock pools in beaches everywhere.

Did you know?

...that clownfish live in anemones with long wavy arms. These ideal hiding places mean bigger fish can't find and eat them.

Courtney the Clownfish Fairy

and her tiny helper Tickle glide through the tropical waters, helping out creatures in trouble.

49

Stargaze Surprise

When Kirsty and Rachel went to Camp Stargaze, they were over the moon to meet the seven Twilight Fairies. Each of the tiny new friends lit up the night sky with their fizzing wands and trails of stardust. Just watching them flicker in the evening air made the girls' hearts flutter with excitement!

It's all been so exciting, the Twilight Fairies' names have got in a muddle. Can you work out who is who? Unscramble the letters, then write the correct name next to each of Kirsty and Rachel's glittering new friends.

SAIMEI

Maisie

THE MOONBEAM FAIRY

NAARSIB

Sabrina

THE SWEET DREAMS FAIRY

MAGORN

Morgan

THE MIDNIGHT FAIRY

AAV

Ava

THE SUNSET FAIRY

AZAR

Zara

THE STARLIGHT FAIRY

XIEL

Lexi

THE FIREFLY FAIRY

SANMIY

Yasmin

THE NIGHT OWL FAIRY

ers can be found on page

Meet Penny
the Pony Fairy

Draw Glitter nuzzling up to her Pet Keeper Fairy.

Personality

Sweet and shy, but sometimes happy-go-lucky too!

I'll always thank Kirsty and Rachel for rescuing my magical party bag from Jack Frost and his goblins!

Animal Companion

Glitter. She's an enchanted pony with a brilliant ice-white coat!

Favourite colour

Fresh, snowy white.

Favourite thing about ponies

Their swishy manes and tails. Silver swirls burst from Glitter's fur when Penny brushes her!

Yummiest food

Apples, mints and sugar cubes.

Most trusted magic

Glitter has a magical aura that other ponies in the human world can sense too.

When Glitter is fairy-size, the little pony is no bigger than a dandelion. Her horseshoes are said to bring bags of luck – fairies like to fix one on the front door of their toadstools.

I found Glitter on page ......

Fairy outfit

Penny's turned-up jeans are just right for riding in. She teams them with knee-high boots and a matching belt. When she gets dressed, she brushes her golden curls into two tumbling bunches. Her lovely purple necklace was a present from Bella the Bunny Fairy.

Whiskers, Wands & Waggy Tails

The Pet Keeper Fairies are delighted to be reunited with their beloved pets! Now all the animals and their keepers are getting ready to scamper back to the safety of Fairyland. Take a peep out of your window before you go to sleep tonight and you might just spot them tumbling happily through the sky!

$$\frac{1}{7}$$

Thank you so much for getting the Fairies and their pets back together again – where would they be without you? All the folk of Fairyland wish you lucky days, dreamy nights and a heart that's always filled with magic!

Kirsty x
and
Rachel x

Glitter

A

Sunny

B

Flash

C

D

Sparky

Twinkle

E

Mistey

F

Shimmer

G

Glitter — A

Sparky — D

Twinkle — E

Sunny — C

Misty — F

Flash — C

Shimmer — G

Can you count up all seven of the magical pets? Match each animal to its tracks...

60

Answers can be found on page

Answers

Page 7 – Enchanted Pet S.O.S

MISTY	– on page 10
GLITTER	– on page 19
SHIMMER	– on page 35
SPARKY	– on page 41
FLASH	– on page 47
TWINKLE	– on page 55
SUNNY	– on page 57

Page 8 – Shivery Spot-the-Difference

Page 20 – Super Sporty Wordsearch!

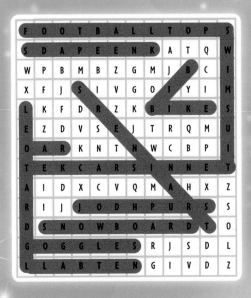

Page 21 – Sweet Little Mystery

The mystery fairy is Juliet the Valentine Fairy.

Page 34 – Words and Wishes

Chrissie says: "My magical objects are a card, a carol sheet and a spoon."

Page 47 – Flowery Fairy Fun

Page 58 – Stargaze Surprise

AVA THE SUNSET FAIRY
LEXI THE FIREFLY FAIRY
ZARA THE STARLIGHT FAIRY
MORGAN THE MIDNIGHT FAIRY
YASMIN THE NIGHT OWL FAIRY
MAISIE THE MOONBEAM FAIRY
SABRINA THE SWEET DREAMS FAIRY

Page 60 – Whiskers, Wands & Waggy Tails

A – GLITTER
B – SUNNY
C – FLASH
D – SPARKY
E – TWINKLE
F – MISTY
G – SHIMMER

Meet all the Rainbow Magic fairies in these exciting storybooks!

The Rainbow Fairies

Ruby the Red Fairy - 978-1-84362-0167
Amber the Orange Fairy - 978-1-84362-0174
Saffron the Yellow Fairy - 978-1-84362-0181
Fern the Green Fairy - 978-1-84362-0198
Sky the Blue Fairy - 978-1-84362-0204
Izzy the Indigo Fairy - 978-1-84362-0211
Heather the Violet Fairy - 978-1-84362-0228

The Weather Fairies

Crystal the Snow Fairy - 978-1-84362-633-6
Abigail the Breeze Fairy - 978-1-84362-634-3
Pearl the Cloud Fairy - 978-1-84362-635-0
Goldie the Sunshine Fairy - 978-1-84362-641-1
Evie the Mist Fairy - 978-1-84362-636-7
Storm the Lightning Fairy - 978-1-84362-637-4
Hayley the Rain Fairy - 978-1-84362-638-1

The Party Fairies

Cherry the Cake Fairy - 978-1-84362-818-7
Melodie the Music Fairy - 978-1-84362-819-4
Grace the Glitter Fairy - 978-1-84362-820-0
Honey the Sweet Fairy - 978-1-84362-821-7
Polly the Party Fun Fairy - 978-184362-822-4
Phoebe the Fashion Fairy - 978-184362-823-1
Jasmine the Present Fairy - 978-1-84362-824-8

The Jewel Fairies

India the Moonstone Fairy - 978-1-84362-958-0
Scarlett the Garnet Fairy - 978-1-84362-954-2
Emily the Emerald Fairy - 978-1-84362-955-9
Chloe the Topaz Fairy - 978-1-84362-956-6
Amy the Amethyst Fairy - 978-1-84362-957-3
Sophie the Sapphire Fairy - 978-184362-953-5
Lucy the Diamond Fairy - 978-1-84362-959-7

The Pet Keeper Fairies

Katie the Kitten Fairy - 978-1-84616-166-7
Bella the Bunny Fairy - 978-1-84616-170-4
Georgia the Guinea Pig Fairy - 978-1-84616-168-1
Lauren the Puppy Fairy - 978-1-84616-169-8
Harriet the Hamster Fairy - 978-1-84616-167-4
Molly the Goldfish Fairy - 978-1-84616-172-8
Penny the Pony Fairy - 978-1-84616-171-1

The Fun Day Fairies

Megan the Monday Fairy - 978-1-84616-188-9
Tallulah the Tuesday Fairy - 978-1-84616-189-6
Willow the Wednesday Fairy - 978-1-84616-190-2
Thea the Thursday Fairy - 978-1-84616-191-9
Freya the Friday Fairy - 978-1-84616-192-6
Sienna the Saturday Fairy - 978-1-84616-193-3
Sarah the Sunday Fairy - 978-1-84616-194-0

The Petal Fairies

Tia the Tulip Fairy - 978-1-84616-457-6
Pippa the Poppy Fairy - 978-1-84616-458-3
Louise the Lily Fairy - 978-1-84616-459-0
Charlotte the Sunflower Fairy - 978-184616-460-6
Danielle the Daisy Fairy - 978-1-84616-462-0
Olivia the Orchid Fairy - 978-1-84616-461-3
Ella the Rose Fairy - 978-1-84616-464-4

The Dance Fairies

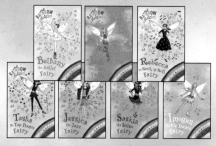

Bethany the Ballet Fairy- 978-1-84616-490-3
Jade the Disco Fairy - 978-1-84616-491-0
Rebecca the Rock 'n' Roll Fairy - 978-1-84616-492-7
Tasha the Tap Dance Fairy - 978-1-84616-493-4
Jessica the Jazz Fairy - 978-1-84616-495-8
Saskia the Salsa Fairy - 978-1-84616-496-5
Imogen the Ice Dance Fairy - 978-1-84616-497-2

The Sporty Fairies

Helena the Horseriding Fairy - 978-1-84616-888-8
Francesca the Football Fairy - 978-1-84616-889-5
Zoe the Skating Fairy - 978-1-84616-890-1
Naomi the Netball Fairy - 978-1-84616-891-8
Samantha the Swimming Fairy - 978-184616-892-5
Alice the Tennis Fairy - 978-184616-893-2
Gemma the Gymnastics Fairy - 978-184616-894-9

There is a book of fairy fun for everyone.

www.rainbowmagicbooks.co.uk